Mommy's SMILE

Written by Lenora L. Wright

Illustrated by Ros Webb

Copyright © 2021 Lenora L. Wright.

All rights reserved. This book is protected by the copyright laws of the United States of America. No part of this book may be reproduced or transmitted in any manner without written permission of the copyright owner. Permission may be granted upon request.

To my dearest son, who came into the world with the fullest intent of his mother's love. But mommy didn't know she was going to struggle once you graced this world with your presence. But lucky for us we had people around us that recognize mommy wasn't smiling anymore and did their best to help mommy with their gentle love and patience. I still remember your first smile at me and I smiled back.

To the Mom who may have lost her smile after your little love entered the world. To the Mommy who struggles with maintaining her happiness. To the Mother who bends from the weight of it all...You're not alone. Your smile is still there and it's BEAUTIFUL.

"Mommy leaves today to have a baby, I'm going to be a big sister"

"Yeah!!! He's here"

"My baby brother is six days old....
but mommy isn't smiling".

"I'm going to be mommy's big helper today"

"I made something for mommy today, ... she didn't smile...I'm not smiling either"

"Mommy is crying, I got help."

"Mommy is going to the doctor today"

"Daddy says mommy just needs some rest."

"Mommy smile today"

"...and so did I"

About the Author

Lenora L. Wright is a daughter, sister, wife and mother. Who was blessed to birth 2 little souls into the world. In doing so, she learned that there is a fourth trimester. A fourth trimester of adjusting and learning through the ups and downs.

Lenora is a postpartum advocator and wants people to know that postpartum doesn't always look the same for everyone. Her hope is that support and protection is extended past the birth.

"Sometimes love comes before bond and that's OK."
- Lenora L. Wright
Sincerely.mommyhood@gmail.com

Made in the USA
Columbia, SC
11 November 2022